Bennett Cerf's
Book of
LAUGHS

●

Illustrated by
CARL ROSE

Beginner Books
A DIVISION OF RANDOM HOUSE

This title was originally catalogued by the Library of Congress as follows: Cerf, Bennett Alfred. Book of laughs. Illustrated by Carl Rose. [New York] Beginner Books [1959] 61. p. illus. 24 cm. ([Beginner books] B-11) PZ8.7.C4Bo 59—13387 ISBN 0-394-80011-7 ISBN 0-394-90011-1 (lib. bdg.)

One day Marvin went to a farm.

"Would you like to take this
hen home to eat?" the farmer
asked Marvin.

"Oh, I would, I would!" said
Marvin. "But tell me—what does
it eat?"

At the farm Marvin saw a cow.

"What are those two things on
her head?" he asked.

"Those are horns," said the
farmer.

Just then the cow went "Moo."

"Say!" said Marvin. "Which one
of those horns did she blow?"

Another day
Marvin ran into
his house. He
let a fly come in.

Then Marvin
ran out of the
house.
He let in
another fly.

Marvin ran into
the house again.
Another fly
came in.

At last his
mother said,
"Marvin, I wish
you would not
run in and out
of the house. I
do not like all
of these flies in
here."

Marvin said,
"All right,
Mother, show
me which flies
you do not like,
and I will make
them go out."

Marvin went over to play with
Sammy. "What time is it?"
asked Sammy.

"I do not know," said Marvin,
"but I know it is not five yet."

"How do you know it is not
five yet?" asked Sammy.

"Because," said Marvin, "Mother
said I must be home at five. I
am not at home, so it can not
be five yet."

Marvin got a new watch.

Jenny asked him, "Does
your watch tell the time?"

"No, it never tells the
time," said Marvin. "I
have to look at it."

"Mother," said Marvin, "Andy and I want to play elephants, and we want you to play with us."

"How can I play elephants with you?" his mother asked.

"Oh, you can," said Marvin.

"You can play the nice lady

who gives us peanuts."

That night, Marvin was in bed. His mother called up to him: "Marvin, did you put out the light?"

Marvin said, "How would I know? It is too dark here for me to see the light."

The next day Marvin asked his teacher, "Would you be mad at me for something I did not do?"

"Why no, Marvin, I would never be mad at you for something you did not do."

"That is good," said Marvin,
"because I did not do my
homework."

"Marvin," his teacher said, "If
I lay one egg here and another
egg there, how many eggs will
there be?"

Marvin said, "There will not
be any eggs."

"No eggs!" his teacher said.
"Why not?"

"Because," Marvin said, "you
can not lay eggs."

On the way home Jenny said,

  "Marvin, look at my
grandmother.
She went in to get her hair cut.
Now, she will not look like an
old lady any more."

"I can see that," said Marvin.

"Now she looks like an old

man."

One day Marvin had his hand
on the wall of a house. A lady
asked him, "Why do you have
your hand on the house like
that?"

"I have to have
my hand here,"
said Marvin.
"I have to hold
the house up."

"Hold the house
up? That is not
funny," the lady
said. "Go on
home!" So——

Marvin did — and the house
fell down!

The next day Marvin fell in a
lake.

A man saw him fall in and
came to get him out.

The man asked him, "How did
you come to fall in?"

"I did not come to fall in,"
said Marvin. "I came to fish."

That night Marvin ran to his father.

"Father," he called, "Andy just swallowed my ten cents!"

So father shook Andy.

He shook him —

and shook him —

and shook him ——

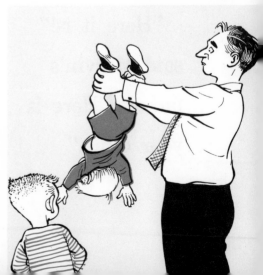

At last a dime
came out of his
mouth.

"Here it is!"
said Marvin's
father. "Here is
your dime."

30

"But this is not my dime," said
Marvin. "Andy swallowed ten
pennies!"

"Marvin," his mother said, "put your shoes on!"

So Marvin put his shoes on.

Then his mother said, "Look here, Marvin. You did not put your shoes on the right feet!"

"But, Mother," said Marvin, "I
do not have any other feet to
put them on."

One day, Marvin did not clean
his room. His mother said,
"Look at this room.
Just look at all this dust!

Why, you can
write your name
on this with
your finger."

"It is good that
I can write it
with my finger,"
said Marvin. "I
do not know how
to write it with
a pencil!"

One day his teacher said,

"Marvin, here is an elephant.

Can you tell us where we find

elephants?"

Marvin said, "We do not have
to find elephants. They are so
big they never get lost."

Marvin made a picture. It had lots of colors. A lady came over to see it.

"Oh, what nice colors!" said the lady.

"Your red is so nice. Your blue is so nice! I wish I could take those nice colors home with me."

"You will," said Marvin. "You
just sat down on them."

The next day, Marvin ran over
to a man and said, "Mr. Smith,
your house is on fire!"

The man
jumped up

and ran,

and ran,

and ran.
And——

——Then he stopped and he said,

"Why did I run?

My name is not Smith! My
name is Jones!"

Marvin sat on the steps of a house.

A man came up to Marvin and asked,

"Boy, is your mother at home?"

"Yes," said Marvin, "she is at home."

"Good," said the man, "then I will

ring the bell."

So he rang the
bell, but no one
came. He rang
the bell again,
but still no one
came.

He rang again
and again and
again and again
and again and
again but no one
came. Then——

He said to
Marvin, "Boy, did
you tell me your
mother was at
home?"

"Oh, yes,"
Marvin said, "she
is at home."

"Then why does
she not come to
the door when
I ring?"

"Because," Marvin said, "she is
not here. This is not my house."

One cold day, Marvin ran out with a shovel.

"Where are you going with that shovel?" his father asked.

Marvin said, "A boy fell in the snow up to the top of his shoes. I am going to dig him out."

His father said,
"He is in the
snow just up to
the top of his
shoes? Why
must you dig
him out? He can
walk out."

"Not this boy,"
said Marvin.
"He fell in head
first."

Marvin had on his good pants.
He was going out with a pail.
His mother asked, "Where are
you going with that pail?"

"I am going to get some snow,"
said Marvin.

"What?" said his mother. "In your good pants?"

"Oh no, Mother," said Marvin. "In my pail."

That day Marvin
came home from
a party.

He said to his
mother, "I had
a lot of ice
cream and cake
at the party.
The ice cream
was so good I
took some for
you."

Then Marvin put his hand in
his pocket.

"That is funny," he said. "Now
where is that ice cream I put
in my pocket for you?"

Sammy told Marvin, "One time
my father shot an elephant in
his pajamas."

Marvin asked,
"How did the
elephant ever
get into your
father's pajamas?"

One day at the
zoo, his father
asked Marvin,
"Do you know
why we call this
a giraffe?"

Marvin said,
"Because he has
a big, long
neck."

His father said, "Why would
his long neck make us call him
a giraffe?"

"Well," said Marvin, "did you
ever see a giraffe with a short
neck?"

Marvin gave a kangaroo some peanuts.

Then the kangaroo jumped
right out of his pen. He jumped
far away . . .

A man ran up and asked Marvin,

"What did you do to make that

kangaroo jump so far?"

"I just gave him some peanuts," said
Marvin.

"Then give me some peanuts, too,"
said the man. "Because——

——"I have to go and get that kangaroo back!"

Marvin was at Sammy's house.

"I have to go home now," said Marvin.

"Do come again," said Sammy's mother. "We would like to see more of you."

"How can you see more of
me?" asked Marvin. "This is all
there is of me. There is no more
of me."